D P R

3 P 2

D 3 R

Published: My Site Dot Com

ISBN: 978-1-7378076-3-6

Published in the USA 2021

Preface
Matrix 1
Apocalypse 9
Pappa Why Are You Walking Up And Down? 19
THE THIRD ARTIST A Short Story From The Book 20
Letter To Mary Ellen 55
Never Build Roads 58
About The Author 59
About The Editor 61

"The danger in creating programs, platforms, and manifestoes lies in attempts to form a cosmic logic. The interior contradiction buried in any manifesto, including any thoughts voiced here, is a virus which goes to work destructively the moment the thought is born. Thus, the more undigested, the less "understood" a program is, the greater the chance for its survival." - Carl Fernbach-Flarsheim

The stories, the short poem, and the letter are a progression of thoughts and reactions to experiences, and memories, that describes a life trajectory that brought a sense of completion in one artist's life and hopefully opens the door to a new generation to consider the behavior of the human mind, the physical and the spiritual.

The concept of the material and personal popularization may in one sense may be irrelevant at the time of its undertaking, becomes the ultimate creative structure equally recognized as ever-shifting time presents its own truth.

MATRIX

"One hundred appeared on the hills that surrounded the valley. Each hill gave way and then came to an end. Now there was none left except the leader, and five thunders came from inside of him. Then he too was gone. Only sparrows remained to fight each other in the bushes..."

He put down his pen. This wasn't at all what he had meant to say. This had come about differently. His hand had written, but where did the thoughts originate? Were they even thoughts? The sentences had written themselves... and they were nonsense.

He picked up the pen once more, "A woman, a man, a child appeared. Those were the only reality. The birds had become transparent reflections, like passersby in a store window..."

He looked startled at the written page; then got up and went to the bathroom sink. He poured himself a glass of water and looked at his reflection in the small mirror. There was a bare light bulb and the dirty knotted cord that hung from the fixture. Cold light flattened the hard features of a thin face and filled in the deep eye sockets.

He had rented this small and ancient apartment in the lower part of Manhattan, one of the few old houses that had been left standing, picturesque to those that didn't have to inhabit them. The rest of the city was a vast concrete park of pavements interspersed by small mounds that were the entrance to the air conditioned underground dwellings and thoroughfares. After three hundred years of misuse, the atmosphere was just beginning to clear. Some adventurous souls, like himself, had started crawling to the surface again; winter bears after a hundred years of hibernation. Mostly they were writers and artists - - Noah sending out the doves in hope they would return with the green-leafed twig.

He went back to his desk in front of the large bay windows. The noon sun was flooding the study with dark orange light that gave it the appearance of a stage in a theater long forgotten. Again he looked down on the paper. It was to have been a score for voice and computer display console. His collaborator, an engineer, had furnished the patterns from galactic rhythms he had observed three years ago.

Thoughtfully he stared at the console of the small computer he had built into a corner of the room. The screen was empty awaiting to be fed the new program. Once more he tried to arrange his thoughts as he placed them on the score-form.

"DIMENSION GALAXY (700), FSHARP (400)," he wrote in the archaic programming language, poetry of the past, "VOICE(50)... there came five out of the wilderness, four gaunt from salvation..." This was not poetry. The program was being superseded be a hand which seemed independent of his brain. The fingers were writing some apocalyptic vision from the outside - - was it from the outside?

The gong and then his wife's voice calling his name at the front door of the apartment. He felt a momentary urge to hide - - the unknown and familiar pursuer.

"I brought you a little friend. I found that one outside our door." She was carrying a scraggly kitten, which was looking at him silently, two oval beads inside black fur. "There's Siamese in that one somewhere - - - cries like a baby."

The little cat kept staring at him, a silent partnership between him and the animal. It seemed as if they had been through a common experience together - - something he was beginning to treasure and which he was unwilling to share.

He laughed uneasily, "A pet in the house. All we need. Somebody to tear up scores on my desk."

His wife bent down and placed the little black cat gently on the floor. It slunk under the console with a small noise that came from deep inside its throat. Two eyes started blinking out of the shadows.

"You have an appointment at three, at the Artcon," she reminded him, "I just spoke to McCloud. They'll be scatter-testing your poetics for random emissions. He asked if you could come a little early; he has something to discuss with you."

A look of annoyance. This will be another political examination, subtly hidden under an innocent conversation covering subjects far removed from his study, where windows opened to sun and sky.

She picked up a tray of burned out steamers and disappeared into the kitchen quarters, that have been converted into an up-to-date food-prep, closed the door gently behind her. When that look came to her husband's face, it was best to cut off. She had learned this during nine years of marriage, lately much disrupted by anxiety. It had taken much courage to burst out of the underground cocoon. A butterfly's wings must unfold before it can take to the air. The butterflies below were in children's books and collections.

The composer settled down once more behind his desk, but work now seemed out of the question. Something chaotic has taken hold of him. He looked at the little black animal under the console. The cat had not moved. Its shining eyes had been following him everyplace. Now it stalked warily from under the console towards where he was sitting; emitting a crackling purr it jumped, landed on his lap. He made no attempt to chase it away.

Two hours had passed. Now he was entering the eletube to be whisked to the Artcon's Anacoustic Laboratories. McCloud looked up from the report that was lying in front of him, as the composer entered the office. He seemed pleased to see him.

"They are still setting up for the scatter-test. As soon as they're ready they'll let us know. Have a seat. - - Tea?"

He pushed forward a cup filled with steaming liquid and settled back comfortably in his chair. "They're after us again. - - The College of Politics has noted that some of your rhythms are identical with patterns that are useable in diplomacy with one of the African nations. They want me to feel you out. Would you be interested in taking a little leave from your work? The government would like you to join a mission there. Some trade negotiations, I believe."

The composer looked at him. He was dumbfounded. A cold anger began to rise which must be carefully controlled. Never before had they been this obvious.

"This is a strange request. I'm sure it must be known that my capacity in that field is for all practical purposes non-existent. Our policies are built on practical governments." He laughed, trying to sound innocently amused, "Government by intuition went out when the computer came in. "I'm sure this direction couldn't have come from very high up. After all, the patterns they speak of are there. They're already using them. Of what use could I be to them, just because I coincidently use the same configurations?"

On the wall the video lit up. The head of a gray-haired technician appeared on the screen. He recognized the composer with a friendly nod; then looked at the other.

"We'll be ready in about five minutes, Mr. McCloud."

"We're on our way," McCloud rose from his seat; both start moving toward the door.

"I saw your wife today, she must have told you. I understand you're deeply involved with experimental scores interweaving cosmic patterns with the human voice."

The composer grunted noncommittally, "It's just a beginning... a very beginning."

The two men left the room and stepped on the broad rollway platform that was to carry them to the scatter-testing labs.

Three more hours had to pass. Then he was back in his study. An urgency now took hold of him. His head ached, a pounding that bordered on migraine.

"RANDOM(50)..." he forced himself to write, "MATRIX (7), X(100)..." a desperate hope, then his hand numbed.

"Five entered..." it wrote, "Five were born, so that four could witness, in the beginning...

in the very beginning...

APOCALYPSE

This is the word that I speak. Take all that is hollow into the washbasin. Take all that is flat where I have seen what is new. Bring all where I've seen the master assemble the fragments into one. Solidify those matters, both large and small, into what is belonging into the parts broken forever and not held in place and those that have given me absolute power into which I wrap myself and those which I have become in my solidity for all to hold.

This is the meaning of all that is held in my hand be it in the right or the left: Fold that which is given to be held into two, fold it into twice the holding power so that it may move from right to left, to go again to the right. Hold that which is begun from the holder of all broken shards so that I can see where all is held away from the master-tribe, the ones that begin to break what is not begun to heaven, not also that which is open. To the tribes I shall speak.. to them hearing what has been kept from my sons to those who never hold what is enriched in wilderness begun and ended there.

This is it's meaning from that begun, ended broken hold-of by me so I can spear the token that has been given to me for all ages. For a thousand this has been brought about, for thousands this is overcome in heaven or in hell, so that I can be settled in the outer reaches from where I can be seen.. for all this is hindered by the others from the other reaches of totality. Totality is met up with, not on the plains of the outer limits but in the stripes of yonder years that I can still enumerate from those toll-free houses on which I stand to be outfoxed by my inner self. This is the nature of the civilizations of mankind: Come to the other hindquarter of the calf, the golden hind of which they speak when they cannot affirm me or deny.

This is the totality as seen through the looking-glass of memories gone far by.. totality is the rational of those then that have not yet overcome who I am in all my clothing, in which I appear to them. Totality to them is not forbidden by me or any other apparition in their dreams.. totality is the great water which they have to cross in order to appear before themselves as they are in this reality of realities. This I can now evaluate when it's overcome by me so they can be after-brought to the manure-pile of holiness that those that cannot speak can fulfill at their own leisure. Toward them that have, give even more. Civilization is that. All civilization of those that call themselves man, that call themselves woman. Take away what has been given and then call yourself what is left. That is the space I occupy for now and forever.

Forward and backward is the totality begun and ended. So is the total being in the ruse of a hermit begun and ended. This is the nail on which it's hung. For this is the hanging garden of all the missions that man is heir to. This is his alternating trade on which he hangs his act. For this you are given the act of numerologist.

Toward none of these am I believing the truth. Toward all of them I have gained another tribe with which it can hold together.. this is as it must be for always as I am beholden to the other forces that can give me the hold over my own domain. For this is not in the interest best for all mankind. This is not in keeping with what I have given to the other side of myself.

Fortitude, this is what the other side has given to my inner teaching, has given to me if not them that haven't been called upon to perform the outright follow-up. Together, fortitude and outside-image, is the formalization of all that I can perform, now and forever thereafter.

For in this house as in all the other houses the man is called to perform inside of his own image and woman is his other side. For in this house woman is meant to perform inside of herself and man is her other side. These are the tablets on which I have written the matters for all to see. Mankind and womankind are one in love for all to see, that I have written on those images that I have called mankind..

meant to be called humanity. That was the lie from the beginning: mankind··· And reality: humanity··· was the finality and shall be so.. this I am now.. so.

The house-holds of two of the middle station is given to me for the outer rim on which I can be given outer aid. This is to be harbored for many years of toil from which I can gather what has been brought into the domain from other reaches of the imprisonment. This cannot be so entitled by any other means since I cannot be given the other side's values.

Forward going I cannot be interested in the out layer in which I have wrapped the inner tube which is myself. So that in other layers I can be knighted, this is where I customarily lie, in between the toes of the crocodile. Toward nothing am I driven··· toward the all sustaining nothing-vessel. Coming from the body from the outside into the inner space, this is the brought-about rescue. This is the sound which I hold in holiness the one that has come to me from the outer reaches of being, this is the outer manifestation.

Toward nothing am I pressed more deeply than my outer sounds can bring me: To the inner sounds, -U and I –one always coming, the other going, one:

Akk, the other: One. This is the container from which I feed, husk that I mean to destroy when I become who I am··· in every direction.

In this situation I am the clear-maker to my own inner brothers that fulfill my inner needs as I bring them about, one after the other. This is the other side of which I am speaking. This is what issues from the mouth and is vibrating inside the head, but not in the same manner as U and I··· which are farther inside from where I speak. Let me listen as I hold the finger pressed against the ear.

Forward is this begun and not so brought about by the other perimeters which I have given over to myself. So is this begun under more moderate circumstances under which I am leaning against the supporting wall, myself.

For myself I have given the outside in which I am wrapped, in which I have given in turn the other perimeters to the others that follow me and to those now surrounding me. To the other side I can give what has been bought with the better part of my self, the part which I can touch with one hand. So this is not so caught by surprise as I may have seen it in previous encounters. To the other side I can give what has been seen in other lands and other laces of servitude of my inner being. So is this not so easily followed by my inner master. To that I can never bring myself to see what comes from behind.

Come to my other parts on which I have gained no such things as are manifest in the other regions. To them I can never be certain until I have forgiven what has been told me from other times and places. Such a man cannot be forgetting what he has to learn in other times from which he comes into this world. Stop to clarify. Such is the outer layer, not yet begun to bring forth the rest of the seeds, not valued by me or the others. Carry the outer layer around with you? Until it has begun to issue its brood..? Forth from here, I come. To the end from which I can see what keeps itself hidden to my ears, the sound that stretches from here to there. Stop to clarify··· Not yet begun to be heard··· Too early when carried around with me in that net-full of gasping fish choking to death for lack of air, even so surrounded by it.

Total the whole earth on which we inhabit the spots that it is made of, those manifestations on which

I can browse to my heart's content until it's my time to leave. Total it in the whole hand of my being and you find no other kind of manifestations like this in the universe that I have spawned. Earth is Earth only no matter where we find it. Don't look for it among the stars, it's already here to be grasped. Wherever I go it goes, it's the life-support system that follows me to and through the stars. It's my body, though time.

Brought about by the far distant lands that I inhabit, I cannot bring the inner thought into the foreground since it isn't in the same room that I'm inhabiting this moment. So far is the distance that I am not able to inhabit the outer perimeters in the full glory that behooves it to be, to be inhabited. So far am I from the inner me that I cannot even see the light in which I stand. Thus I am not able to inherit was has been left to me by all my ancestors to be dealt with by me in this body only. This is the inner man speaking.

Brothers, together we bring forth what has been for all to hear. To all of them in whom we confide our inside feelings, to whom we give the inherited outside temple of our being; to them there is no such temple given but from the outside. Toward all my inner brothers I stand in my shirt all but naked to be held by them, on my inner table where the bowls of fruit ripening await now to be eaten at a later date. To all of these, give what can be given now at this time for all to be obtained, by all appreciated in times to come. So is the name which we give to be spoken in the real tongue of humanity: KA NA. Await the name, await the outer glory which I can give you which you perceive as given from outside the cloak in which I wrap myself··· to be felt.

For the old ones have not even begun to speak to me in the outer layer of my being. That has not been taken in by the others that come into those outer layers to speak of what I have been. Speak of what I have begun, speak of what I have to be. Tall this man stands. Taller the woman on high heels? Total; not like this one··· too tall.

Totality does not come in pairs··· and proof is not needed there. Comes from where the outer layer is not yet turned on··· energized. From there where I have not yet begun nor have I spoken from that place so is this other mechanism set in motion. To all begun and never ended, so am I in the outer layer begun, never ended. To all seen like that.

For this one I am in the hold of the great ship on which I have arrived in the land of the lotus eaters. To find them in this clothing I have to initiate what cannot be begun without my ten fingers. To find them I cannot be so inflamed with passion that I cannot see the flame from afar. Trapped in that trunk of the great beast I am forever beholden to the inner sense… to show me the way out from what and where I have begun to "understand."

Come to this country on which my soul stands in the outer manifestation. To there where I am in hiding from my outside and inner forces which hold me in attention-position. Come now in the outer layers on which I cannot even now behold what I cannot see in the outer eyes that are carried with me on all my voyages. "So far – so good," I now say to this machine in which I appear to every other man and women, "I cannot go farther that tis place today. This is where we have arrived for now, for today."

PAPPA, WHY ARE YOU WALKING UP AND DOWN?

Pappa, why are you walking up and down?

I'm thinking.

What are you thinking?

I'm wondering why God made us look just like Him.

I know why.

So, tell me.

Because He doesn't like us to look like anybody else except Him.

Oh, you are so right. How come I didn't think of that. You are so smart.

Pappa, so now why are walking up and down?

I'm wondering how come you are so smart.

I know why.

So, tell me.

Because God made me that way.

Of course, you are so right.

Pappa, so why are you still walking up and down?

THE THIRD ARTIST

A short story from the book

Yesterday I wasn't sure. Today I'm sure! Tomorrow I may know more. I'll let you know if I've made a mistake.

It was all clear to me when I came out to the mountains. Now the thoughts I felt there are already beginning to blur. Even down here, still almost seven thousand feet above sea level, it's beginning to do that. The letters and the pages they're written on. Letters are made in the unfinished world of our civilization, our philosophies, religions, myths, books, sciences, and symbols. Truth only dimly perceived in a perpetual semi-darkness.

I have a young friend, he cures people. "My hand" he says, "is the tool of the universe, whose energies synchronize with those of the sick. I pray to my creator. But when I fold my hands in front of my chest, it is to sense my inner center, not to ask favors." He recognizes this. Still not all his patients are cured. Others quit his treatment to early.

It's a little too early in Spring. The mountains are cold. I sit in meditation, but not long enough, and then I work in the earth with a kitchen scraper found in the car. I try to concentrate on the void, on nothing. Thoughts come anyway. I try not to let images hold me. That is the exercise.

Sand and rocks make small landslides that keep pushing the sand back, trying to refill the cavities that I dug, still I make progress. The wind throws sand around me in gusts, and I try to listen without letting it take hold of me. Two small birds fly down to look but remain at a safe distance. It's really too cold but I have the feeling I'm on the right track. I get a thought, "Make a sand box." Later, driving home I get another thought. "Let the earth be my sand box."

The disease and the cure. When it is the disease, I call it Yomotsu-kuni, the foreign lands. When it's the cure, I call it Takamahala, the square encased by four directions. Both names are vibrations that come out of my mouth and are heard by the ears. A few years ago, I wrote a small book. That book was easier to write. My world then was a kind of matrix, a womb of related decisions, for which I had attempted to find a structure. Soon I was deeply disturbed by this floating net I had created, without center, and without a source.

At that time I met my teacher.

Now I must be more careful. The subject covers a broader horizon and I must be careful. Before I write further, I'd better dig deeper, so that I learn how to say it.

Easter Sunday. I try to dig again near where I'd dug before. A little platform of earth inside a small arroyo, then a small cliff and a hill covered with mountain junipers. First I just sit there and let my voice come out of me. The cry of the newborn, sensei calls it. "Suuu – A-Wa." Inside "Su," I find peace. I used to think of it as the voice of Yomotsukuni searching for Takamahala. I still think so.

Peace is not where the poet is looking for it. It's neither above nor below. Neither inside nor outside. It's not like that. The Garden of Eden in not a direction. I dig a little deeper than the last time. Then I place five large pebbles on a little mound next to the hole··· eight pebbles in a row next to that.

Next afternoon. I find the hole partially caved in and the eight small pebbles gone. I'm slightly annoyed. Then I remember, I came here to learn how to say it. I dig again. I make things a little more complex and this time I place eight stones in two rows of four each.

It's almost a week later, past the middle of April. There is a garden in back of my house. Yesterday I prepared the soil. This morning I'm putting in seeds. The sun is hot. The wind is cold. This is semi-arid land. Still, some plants will sprout. There were others in that spot before.

Today is a bad day for learning. I'm too sure of what I want to say.

It's evening. I'm told the best time for meditation is early in the morning before sunrise. For me, it's better late at night. We one visited the land of the Hopis, high on top of a mesa. There the sun rises below, and there it was easier in the morning. There I felt the sunlight strike my face like the touch of someone's hand. The sun chief who had invited us was 112 years old and smoked Winston's. He had spent his life awaiting the restoration of Masaw's sacred tablets; the fulfillment of a prophecy, which would bring freedom to his people.

"Let me see this before I die," he said to sensei. It was the wrong time for giving him an answer. Three weeks later he died.

That night an Indian asked, "Do you believe there are flying saucers?" Sensei answered that he'd never seen any. The man said, "We see them all the time. One night one of them came down behind the house at the foot of the mesa. I saw a man come out of it. I called to him to find out if he was hurt but he didn't answer. By the time I'd run into the house to get a flashlight, both man and craft had disappeared."

Sensei asked, "In what language did you call him?"

I called in English.

You should have spoken Hopi.

That's the closest my teacher came to explaining the meaning of word-soul that night. It's hard to teach the Kototama. The Hopi know some of the sounds.

I'm again at my digging place in the arroyo. There are changes where I had dug. Four pebbles had been scattered. Four others now formed a square with a large rock in the center. The original five pebbles had not been disturbed. No doubt, the new arrangement is a better way to say it. I may be ready to say the next thing now. Without getting too precious about all this. All I need to do is to arrange the square a little more precisely. Now, it's like this: Those corner stones are stones, of course. In this language they're also symbols that stand for certain sound vibrations. That beats writing down letters; you can always pick up a stone. Four corner stones; A (aaaaah), O (oh!), U (uuuuh), and I (aigh). And I said, these stones are only symbols.

The center stone is I (eeeeeeh). That's the will to live, without which there is no life itself. Those corner stones are the "mother sounds." The center stone is the parental sound, it's neither male nor female. Without that, not even "nothing" is born. These five sounds n this phonetic order: I, A,O,U,E are Yahweh, sound vibrations which are more than what I hear with my ears. Vast dimensions that are myself from the very beginning.

Today is the last day of April. I went back to the spot and I'm upset by events. I've been advised many times, "Don't get taken over by phenomena." I've been overtaken.

I find that the stones have been moved once more. One stone is missing, the fifth stone. I put all things back in order. This time I make the center stone the larger so there may be no doubt.

It's been almost three weeks since I've been in the mountains. Events in my life seem mostly to circle around finances. The most sophisticated outgrowth of the U-dimension is business. A combination of bad judgement and a bad economy placed our restaurant deep in debt. We have to let our help go and my wife and I must run the business ourselves. Pay back debts.

I'm working eleven hours a day, now. This doesn't leave much time for digging. In any case, digging here is more complicated. It's a space of brick, wood, and concrete – and I am surrounded by solid walls. The mountain has moved, because I've moved the mountain.

It's the end of May. I'm cooking. Eleven hours a day has become thirteen hours, and I am weary to the bone. How do I cut onions? In Japan they cut off both ends, then they cut them in half, then they cut the center. The they cut along the life rings and each piece becomes a small moon. Each piece a new moon, the first sliver in the sky. A beginning. The sound TA but there are many TA's. Ta is a rice field where all seeds are coming up. They are the children. The sound T, the father sound, an action, and the mother sound A, which is a dimension. Which is also my imagination. And I must be careful, even at this early stage. TA is the concept, not the name. To be able to grasp the new moon is never <u>that</u> TA. Sensei just pointed out to me today that my way of speaking is in O-dimension (the intellect) is not very clear.

That's the reason I'm an artist, I guess. Either that or I'm stupid. After all, I'd hate to admit that.

A new prison, I thought. This morning I recognized that I might have misunderstood. Three thoughts passed through me in the shape of three woman: the mother, the sister, and the wife. I held communion with them, and it was Saturday. The sound is A.

It's another Spring, another April. Often now I see three "things" in front of me. One of them, a horse. They're like subtitles on the screen of my everyday life. They help me judge- my yes and my no. Are they hallucinations? Two months later I find a chart in a translation of the Nei Ching, the Yellow Emperor's Classic on Internal Medicine. The chart shows a concordance, a system linking concepts:

Animal: Horse

Organ: Lung and Large Intestine

Color: White

Etc.

Etc.

I hold up the mirror of the Kototama and recognize a dimension. The dimension is U. But those are symbols. U is U.

It's Summer, and the Fourth of July. I'm in the mountains a little higher up, where breathing is hard. I'm sitting in a meadow. Sun patches are crawling towards me, finally pass over me, and the sun bursts over the ridge.

YoKoTaLi

That's the way it comes out of my mouth. I'm in the Pecos Wilderness. There is no dictionary for the Kototama. YoKoTaLi is a group of child sounds born of the parental act. YoKoTaLi is a state of recognition at the moment I utter the sounds Yo- Ko- Ta-Li. "In heaven there are ethereal spirits, upon earth there is form and shape. Yang, the turbid element, returns to earth. In heaven, there are eight regulators. Upon earth there are five principles, and by means these all living creatures can be transformed into parents."

Nei Ching

The Kototama is the principle of the word soul: the marriage of eight father sounds with the five dimensions in which I manifest and produce the child sounds, which are all phenomena I'll encounter in my universe. Four pebbles on the ground: A, O, U, and E. The dimension of judgement is E. Four pebbles lying in a square, a large rock is in the center.

We are standing on a narrow foot bridge over the Santa Fe River. Most of the time the river bed is dry. Sarai looks down where the bed is now covered with beautiful patterns of sand and pebbles formed by the water when the bed is flooded. "this is an image of how the water acts when it runs down there."

"That isn't an accurate picture" I answer, "because, though beautiful, it doesn't give sense of what I experience when water is in action down there. It's an instantaneous image of that action, nonetheless; it's the result up to this moment."

So we argue back and forth. We find ourselves becoming annoyed with each other. As I look over the railing behind me, I noticed a small rivulet of water. The river has suddenly started to run. "This is what I mean!" I'm full of excitement. There's no rain cloud in any direction. I paint water colors. A drop of paint drips on the paper before I start the first stroke. At what point did the painting begin?

At what point starts what? At what point starts creation? Now I paint watercolors, gouache. I find time for this every morning. Its part of my meditation and it's very hard for me. I had to throw out all but the brushes and the paint. When I work like that, something deep inside of me has meant it. I look at what I've done only after I've done with it. There are sounds that appear inside of me when I paint. They are like a title to the strikes, as if something is teaching me a new vocabulary. The images and sounds are not accurate. It's too early for that. But it's closer to the way it must have been in the beginning.

The child sound TE is a vibration on its way to becoming something. My judgement is a sound. I've been told that its color is read. TE belongs to the E dimension but to color it red because I've been told is stupid and a new blockage. It's a misunderstanding of the teaching. Better the wrong color.

On October 19, a young man offered to take my place as cook in the restaurant.

On October 21, I paint two images. Both are aspects of the same thing. I decide to glue them together, one below the other. This may be one reason for the scrolls of the Orient. In the West we discovered the movies.

The sounds for the first paining: Mu KE I GE KO.

The sounds for the second one: U NU ME KE GE KO

The sound and the meaning. The meaning eventually must be absolute as it crosses the dimensions. The memory on which I draw must come from a different area of the O dimension than I'm accustomed to draw from. The A, I understand, is not the A, the O is not the O. Painting is a little easier; there is a little chance to misconstrue it all.

A sweep of the eye

I'm 35

Say something funny.

"I'm allowed…"

Everything is allowed,

To grow.

Say something funnier.

Everything needs love,

All of it.

Boruch…!

I am very ill. A dangerous condition. Everything teaches.

A dangerous illness does it especially well. Listen?

It's not like that.

I have just read the book. And now I know about the father vibrations and the mother dimensions and the phenomena. It's not like that.

The Moslem speaks of Allah, the Jew speaks of his Adonai, the Christian mouths the words of Christ, the Buddhist mumbles "Han Nya Shin Nyo." The experience of one sound is better than the Bible, the Koran, and the whole Mandala of the Kototama thrown in one. The most insignificant of all deities is bigger than anything we can imagine with the intellect. I write in Anger. I just remember that malfunctioning of the liver shows up emotionally as anger. I'm being treated, diagnosis Kidney/LIver is Kio-Zitsu:

Body and Soul.

It's two days later. I'm still very ill. Something like a mild stroke. The body out here.. to experience and to judge. The highest art is judgement. Not the art where something is beautiful, ugly, dirty, successful, painful, sensuous, religious. The judgement of which I speak here recognizes the only sounds possible for this phenomenon at that moment. Not intellectualized, not rationalized, and not proved. There's no sense trying to tell the absolute in languages. Painting is only a puny exercise along the way. Each man's way is paved with such exercises.

To repeat even one for the sake of approval is betrayal. To repeat it for sentimental reasons is lack of judgement. To repeat them without recognizing their love is blockage. We're accustomed to see with the physical eyes. We speak of intuition, but even intuition ultimately takes the road through the physical eye. From there we judge and form and say we mature. But it's right here where the prison walls start. As long as my eyes are closed and something from behind paints on that white sheet, my exercise lies in my ability to stay in contact with this "something." From this ability I derive a new judgement. But once the physical eye has opened, my former judgement overtakes me. To say this is a poor judgement is to miss the point. It's a judgement which is true, but it imprisons me in the lower dimensions of my existence. It's a judgement based in smaller lands.

"Beim Ersten seit ihr frei,

Beim Zweiten seit Ihr Knechte."

- Goethe (Faust)

I speak of A, not of the letter.

Aaaaaah!

A kind of love, blue, its organs are the liver and the gallbladder, my sentiment, my imagination. It's a land bigger then my physical five senses, and bigger than memory.

Let me try again:

It's the light the blind man sees,

In the very beginning.

It sparks the universe and expands to the gates of infinity.. and returns like an arrow to merge once more into chaos.

That's the way I'm able to recognize it within my present awareness.

Stand at Death's door.

Where is the art here?

Even if you were to learn it through me.

Whose Death?

Who is the Father?

I is the human soul.. is I

I love my greenhouse. I love every flower in it.

Who'll love it next?

A-I is the seer of things.

I is the seer of nothing.

My greenhouse, who'll love it next?

We take care, or better, we help take care.

The car cannot say "I drive," once it recognizes its driver.

The point of separation between driver and car is at the point of contact. At that point the car may say "I drive."

At that point stands the Tower of Babel.

Everything is allowed to grow. Everything needs love.

All of it.

I is the seer of U

U is chaos in the pure state.. mistaken as Death

Uuuuuuh is the cry of pleasure and pain.

Five senses.. is U

8 actions

The Father

8 vibrations

Without them I cannot begin to recognize that there are 8

Eight father sounds

In Physics

A Theory

A Nobel Prize

There are 8

We already found them..?

The paint is pushed from behind me. I open my mouth. There are 8. I already know I'll find them at the source. What color is the source? Name the children! There are so many.. children. Yes I know, I already said all this!

Sucked into the abyss

Spewed out once more

My illness is like that

Is this death's door,

Or the entrance to that door?

SU

The ascent from the abyss and

The last step out of chaos

After that the light

SU

In the beginning.. in the very beginning

Let me tell a funny story. This book.

I'm not writing it for entertainment. I'm writing for later, maybe it's already too late. My judgement has not been too good, so maybe it's too late. The trouble is, I just wasn't ready earlier, so I couldn't write until now. I was trying "to make it another way." Now, maybe I'm trying to "make it" for everything except for telling sexy stories, and comparing notes. How's your kidney, your heart, your gallbladder especially?

Let me tell a funny story: waaaaaaaaah!

SU

In the beginning..

A And WA

He Said

Let There Be

Light

Su – A – WA. If A is light in Heaven, the WA forms light on Earth

O is in Heaven WO is on Earth

(oh!) (woe)

E Judgement WE

In Heaven and on Earth

The decision of my ancestors is the direction of mankind. Up until now it was the best way. It's the way they willed it. When there is a change on the offing, the artist is usually the first to feel pain. There is a change in the offing. We've already willed it. Look to the prophecies, whatever the religion. There is another beginning. The artist of the second order, the artist of our civilization feels the pain. The difference between the second and the third artist is a funny story. I must speak about myself, I push upward. I use my illness for leverage. My sins use it to punish me. There is no other punishment. There is love. In the dimension of highest moral judgment, in the sound E, love is absolute.

I speak much about love. Maybe it's because I can't give enough. What do I know of absolute love? I came out of the abyss, out of SU, I came out to experience.. like a probe..? No, more lie a detachable warhead. I cannot continue like this. I must make a stand someplace. If not even at death's door, then where? The opposite of my love is fear. We must all make a stand some place. I must forgive.

"And don't let the cat in the house!"

The Rainbow: "This is the sign of the covenant
That I am giving between me and
Every living soul that is with you.."

Between A and WA are 8 sounds

Between O and WO theer are 8

Between U and WU, eight

Eight between E and WE

"Between me and every living soul"

The children..

32 sounds "To the generations of eternity"

The Holy Spirit.. Eight more vibrations between I and WI.

Any one sound is bigger than a thousand I imagine with the dictionary. I'm not sure this is the right way to say it.

I must try to do this differently:

In the mountain I placed 8 stones

In two rows of four. Those eight

Should have been all one of a kind.

Altogether four kinds. Thirty-two in all

32 stones must be placed there

YE SI TE LE KO, I don't know what this "means," and at this moment I don't really need to know. I have the same feeling when I paint in meditation. I lose this feeling when I open my eyes. Then my judgement is not clear any more, deciding what to do with it. Or for that whether I should do anything with it at all. Funny, just a few days ago, this questioning had already been answered. It's better to go back and set up stones.

We all need to eat, I say, and many want to raise children.. the blind duck leads the ducklings off the road. But nonetheless all of them march.. and books will be written about blind ducks, and books will be read.. and paintings will be painted, and paintings will be hung: all entitled, "So it Goes."

For me it goes no more. There's no advance by marching forward, nor retreat by marching backwards. Advance is a judged recognition, which I achieve when permitted and permission is not granted until I am ready. Who determines when I am ready? The I and then the E. A repetition of many of these two sounds, like a stream of divine sparks, create the child sound YE. There is a deep connection here. This sound and what Moses heard on the Mount. JEHE ASHER JEHE. I am that I am. There is the same connection between this sound and the name of Christ and the name of a Buddhist entity Yezo Busatso. This Bodhisattva is not enshrined in any temple. His shrine can be along the paths as a companion for children to play with.

This sound is in our consciousness whether we're Moslem, Buddhist, Christian, or Hindu. I find it in my own. It has been found by the scientists searching among the mesons and leptons. But it needs to be recognized.

I never mention Simcha, or Stanley, as most people call him. Except for my young friend who cures people, Simcha is my closest friend. His father was an Ethiopian Jew, and a kind of medicine man back in the old country. So Stanley came to a lot of esoteric knowledge at an early age. When he visits me we often spend long hours together and he preaches at me, which temps me to preach back at him. His presence often helps clarify things that I've been told. His knowledge, when I see it through the mirror of the Yatta (the Kototama) reinforces many things that I only vaguely understood before.

I once asked sensei what understand was in Japanese. He laughed, "To understand is under stand in any language."

And here is Stanley. With his eyes boring into me theatrically, he points his finger, "When you had the stroke, who was the first one on whom you called for help··· sensei??"

No, I called on the Father.

It's still early. It's not even that late, come to think of it.

November has just begun. Leaves most fall before the trees are bare and trees must be bare before the crocuses come out. For the artist, it's becoming harder all the time. When the leaves are falling, he's in danger of suicide. He needs at least a religion. Politics is never enough. Or he'd better stay on the perimeter and paint trees, flowers, Indians, and cowboys.. if he's American. The soul is never satisfied with the outer perimeter. We're always boring for the center. But on the road to there we find ourselves surrounded by the synagogues of Satan, mirrors of our own ego. Suicide comes in many forms.

KA SA TA NA HA MA YA LA

Eitgh child-sounds of the A dimension in the order of our technological civilization. This order wasn't invented by Moses not the Greeks, not by Mohammed nor by the Holy Roman Empire. We willed it in all our five dimensions A I U E O. It is the direction of mankind.. the mothers, the fathers, and the children.

There is a road sign ahead: a new direction. Now, after thousands of years we are willing it.

A TA KA MA HA LA NA YA SA.. WA

Eight children of A. Eight sounds in the new order, the third civilization some call it. Another bridge is forming, another covenant between heaven and earth, the rainbow between A and WA. The road is leading through an absolute recognition of the seed from which I sprouted. To arrive at this recognition another kind of evaluation. I must dig a passageway through the mountain of "things" to find the opening from where I can see them being spewed out into my universe.

I find myself stepping on a kind of rolling sidewalk. I step on there with brushes and paper and paints in my hands. Those same hands produce the scenery as the sidewalk rolls by and I get off when my soul gives me a push. I step onto it once more, then again and again. Each time when my hand is permitted to speak, I have all my feelers extended, full concentration. Don't let my eyes divert me into reproducing it all correctly. Try not to let the intellect take over: The "I know what I like." This kind of knowing is like a computer's knowledge. I scan the memory banks and compare everything with what I find in storage there. On this I base my judgement, my yes and my no. What I find in storage there are thousands of years of memory. I find the second civilization with all its suffering, competition, and prisons. Self-imposed prisons, because I willed them so I could recognize the material universe inside of myself and outside of there.

As science is nearing its peak, the artist notices a door, hidden up 'til then. At the very instant of that discovery, the third artist takes his first breath. But he's a long way from maturity.

The colors of the rainbow:

SA is one of the children of A. When SA is born too early, I cannot grasp all those things I see. When SA is born too early, I cannot grasp the Earth and I cannot judge the sky. I can investigate, I can cut apart and separate, and cut again and again, smaller and smaller. I can rationalize things, but my judgement is blind. The SA escapes from the mouth. It's hidden in the word "satisfaction," which I can find in the dictionary. It comes out a kinds of 'sign,' a recognition of everything that has gone on before.

Sensei explains:

He takes hold of his pipe cleaner and throws it on to the rug. He points at the pipe cleaner and then at himself, “Between me and this thing is one direction, a concentrated, total attention, a total expansion is lightening up, between it am myself, between me and this thing is SA.”

Looking in the darkness to catch something.. that’s a definition I find in his writings.

When SA is born too early, not enough has formed to get an accurate picture of WA. WA light up my physical world. When SA is born too early.. Yes, the second civilization is a gruesomely funny story.. I’ve already said it.

A KA SA TA NA HA MA YA LA.. WA

To break out of this order of vibrations needs a lot of work which can’t be done with telescopes and electron microscopes. Which can’t be done by writing this book either.

This book is my exercise in learning how to say it.

My 'art' may or may not include the technology available to me. The point of contact: Nakaima.

Sensei Ogasawara, my teacher's teacher, wrote a message to a student in Sweden. Below are two excerpts:

The starting point of thinking exists in Nakaima, now-here. It does not begin from the history of the past. It cannot be grasped by belief (postulate) in the future either.

As long as one is thinking himself to be a man of some value in this present degenerate world, he can never concentrate in Nakaima.

One thing is certain, at the time of this writing. There is no waiting line at the gate that opens to the third order. When evaluated through the eyes of our present civilization, the entrance fee is too high, and the benefits too uncertain economically. Even when I decide to be very high-minded about all this, I find myself falling into the trap, that's next to the one I've just skirted. Why am I writing this book? No, I mean honestly! As an exercise in judging what I should and should not say.. very commendable! But this morning I said to my wife, "I hope someone will be able to benefit. I'm obliged to speak out before I die." I didn't voice it, but what I meant was: a contribution, something for them to all remember me by.. before I go into oblivion.

"Abandon hope all ye who enter here" is written above the gate that opens to the second order. I was getting ready to march right through it all over again. Will this book be published? The leaves of the tree of life are shaking with laughter. The exercises that I perform no matter what road I've decided them to be. Pure exercise is a group of mirrors which I already know what I'm going to look like when I eventually see myself. That way the mirrors become superfluous. Eventually I'm bound to find there the image I'm looking for: Another great impersonation.

I'm not painting yet.. I still get dizzy when I look down on the paper.. bad liver, bad gallbladder. Both are the A dimension organs, tow sides of the same coin. The five elements of the I-Ching. Wood, Fire, Earth, Metal, Water.. A E I U O. Wood is the mother of Fire for lack of wood the fire dies. Too much wood, same thing. Wood is A, Fire is E.. Natural medicine is based on the I-Ching. Eventually all is based on the Kototama, or word-soul, whatever we decide to call it.

Painter is easier to grasp, writing is easier to understand. Aikido is probably better than both. Sensei asked me yesterday how thick this book will be. I told him that at the moment I'm on page fifty-two, handwritten. Write 1000 pages, he says. Well after 1000 pages I should understand it all. By the time I've done that, I can condense it to maybe.. fifty.. or maybe it's useless altogether.

Let me talk politics.

LETTER TO MARY ELLEN

Dear Mary Ellen,

You sent me a note and your kindest invitation to the exhibit a while ago. You wanted to know what I was doing. I'm in a quandary as to what to tell you. I am only certain of one thing; I am finished with exhibiting because I am finished with symbols. I have found them to be a blind alley. I had to move inside and found there that symbols are another cause of the separation (inside and outside), I'm recognizing now that the road of all of us (the "concrete (?) people") will lead to an eventual recognition of this sooner or later. Yet we were closer to the truth (searching for the thing itself) than the others in the museums and galleries, etc. (ego manifestations, some cry blatant, some more subtle) Our needs are so great and we cast around for solution that are all around us, solutions we are too blocked to see. I said to myself, how can I say we? I am talking about myself – why project this on others.

But I recognize now that what is true for me cannot help but be true for us all. This is just another rationalization for separating myself from the totality – which is an impossibility; a lack of awareness of the nature of the totality. I know now that there is a language – a pre-Babel that exists which has to be rediscovered. The search for it is blocked by the books, exhibits, etc. There are old reference points, fragments of the old civilization out of which we are trying to arise into a new one. The new language is soul to soul – from inside.

There are no books there, no intellectual explanations. It is communication between our seeds which in truth is one seed which we, in our blindness have fragmented by our intellect. I am not denying the intellect, I am only saying that I have to grow beyond it. You may ask, but how do you survive? At the moment Sara and I have a little food shop – which was a plastic donut shop originally when we took it over. I can communicate more easily thru people's stomachs, fewer intellectual blockages then in other areas.

I am surrounded by mountains here. It's easier for me to come to recognition 7,000 feet above sea level: less pollution of all sorts. There's much more I'd like to tell but I am hesitant. It's so easy to be misunderstood – I don't have to tell you. We all wouldn't have become concrete poets if we hadn't found this out – that most painfully. I listen here most intensely to what my mouth is saying in the primitive state.

Keep in touch,

Love Carl

NEVER BUILD ROADS

not not not not not not not but not but not not not not not yet not yet yetnot yet yet not not but yet but not yet but but not but but yet but not yet but yet but not not not not not yet not but gone soon gone free gone free soon gone free free gone gone soon free soon soon free soon gone gone soon free free free never never build roads roads roads roads roads never never never roads build build build build build build roads build build never build never build roads never build never

etc

ABOUT THE AUTHOR

Carl Fernbach-Flarsheim (1921–1992), in 1966 was a Concrete and visual poet whose publications included Uncomputable Poem for Compiler and Poem for Compiler: Version 2 (both 1966) and the loose-leaf collection of poetry and prose fragments From the Designer's Sketchbook (1967). In January 1968 Fernbach-Flarsheim was the subject of a work by Jackson Mac Low that comprised words only made up of letters from his name. It was manifested in black ink on white paper, published as an offset edition, and was also the source of what Mac Low described as a 'verbal musical performance'. In 1970, Carl Fernbach-Flarsheim developed his concepts on The Boolean Image/Conceptual Typewriter

In 1970, Carl Fernbach-Flarsheim (HiKaLu), an artist and college professor began his studies of the Kototama Principle. He moved to Santa Fe in 1972, continuing his studies with Sensei Masahilo Nakazono and applying his art to this Principle. He painted, wrote and provided guidance in Sound Practice exercises.

In the Spring of 1985, Sensei Nakazono, conferred the title of Doctor of Kototama Principle upon him. Doctor HiKaLu is the only person recognized thus far as having earned the rank of Doctor of Kototama Principle. All students of the Life Principle of Kototama are indebted to this man for his efforts. He will always serve as a model of unrelenting dedication to the perfection and purification of one's own substance.

ABOUT THE EDITOR

Dave F. Farbrook (a.k.a. Flarsheim) lived most of his life in New Mexico, with over 25 years of professional experience in research, has compiled a rich anthology of his father's accomplishments and conclusions. Carl Fernbach-Flarsheim wrote his essays, plays, and lectures under his Sage Name, HiKaLu after 1971, when he moved to New Mexico.

This book, The Five Books of Moses, and St. John Transformed can be also referenced in part in The Boolean Theatre, a book written by Dave F. Farbrook on the anthology of his father as a contemporary artist and poet between 1962 through 1985.

Mr. Farbrook has authored essays, a cookbook, a blogsite, and as of this publication, broadcasts with Albuquerque NOW! Podcast.